I0822708

CONTOURS OF THE NEW MILLENNIUM

BY

ANTHONY J. MARLOW

CALIFORNIA

CURRENT FLOW MEDIA LLC

2016

Printed in the United States of America

First Printing, 2017

ISBN 978-0-9986247-5-4

Current Flow Media LLC

731 21st Street, Suite "A"
Paso Robles, CA 93446

CONTENTS

PART 111

PART IV

PART I

PROLOGUE

I was conceived on the Eastern Seaboard during the frost of winter in a land covered with snow and ice. Carried across the great landscape of this country to the Pacific Coast, and transplanted in a paradise of endless summers, earthquakes, and drought. Raised in the tenets of Roman law, only to be formed and shaped by the hand of "Yahve." It is from this evolution of faith, through love and understanding that I now wish to speak. Long passed are the days of hesitation, and the hours of procrastination have run their course. The moment of truth is upon us and destiny shall wait no longer.

I now wish to speak only to those who will listen. But as words are merely the capture of thought, it is my most fervent hope that you will hear what I have to say so that your understanding may prosper into wisdom and that my thoughts and love shall remain but a cherished memory in your hearts. For much have I loved you long before the words had come to me, yet even now those words cannot express the magnitude of that love. Also, to those who have long since departed from us in this life shall I speak; though not to them, but from them and in honor of their memory which will remain forever etched in my heart.

Looking back to the time of my earliest childhood when, with each sunrise, my heart would leap for joy in anticipation of what the new day would bring I must now ask myself: what was this emotion that had so generously come to me and found for itself a home and place to flourish? Was it the folly of a stranger lost in paradise, or simply the desire of a young and restless child in search for the meaning of love? The boy in me that *was* wants to believe the latter, but the man in me that *is* knows better. For love has always been with me since the cradle, and although I am compelled to seek and search further, I find myself no longer lost and seem to have found my way.

For what more can a man ask when all that he will ever need is right there before him. If you would just open your eyes and look, you shall see that love is in the very air we breathe and that paradise is already here waiting patiently for your command. You have often heard it said: "ask and you shall receive." But I believe it to be better stated: "it is there for the taking and one need not ask." For asking implies permission, and since when does one need consent to take what is freely and rightfully his? Such is paradise my friends, and as you will soon discover it is an earthly gift bestowed upon the living; not some intangible thing reserved only for the afterlife.

You have also heard it said: there exists something in store for us in the afterlife, should we either conform or fail to adhere to the mores and teachings of those who have come before us; however, I believe this to be a fiction. For not only is there no afterlife, there is no heaven nor hell either. Having said this, it is not my intention to dislodge you from the faith which you have so devoutly practiced throughout your life, nor deprive anyone of that dream which they have imagined for themselves upon their death; I only wish to give a simple explanation of the concept of *paradise* and how it relates to the here and now.

Let me begin by saying: that you have only this short period of time in paradise to appreciate and understand the meaning of your existence here on earth; the choices that you make which will affect the outcome of your lives, are yours to do with as you will. Have you not heard it said: "today is the first day of the rest of your life"? So choose well my friends, because the consequences thereof which will determine your future depend upon it.

Even though in this life many may have committed numerous

transgressions and injustice against humanity, I believe there is still hope and opportunity for redemption. How so? one might ask. Well, in the first instance, one must understand that he is not the only transgressor that has ever walked the face of the earth. Many have come before you, and there will be others who shall come after. Though it would appear that some present themselves to be above criticism and without blemish, this too is a fiction. For believe me: only those who aspire for truth and humility will unabashedly tell you that they too have committed egregious mistakes, and are not without fault.

Throughout the ages, "too much ignorance has prevailed on this earth and little wisdom has blossomed from it." What I offer today is not wisdom; it is only my most fervent hope that you will step out of the shadow of these failed doctrines and stand before the sunshine of your own conscience and knowledge. It is only through this understanding and belief in yourself, that you will ultimately find the peace and freedom that you now so desperately seek.

In order for you to extricate yourself from the bonds of this nonsense that has for so long enslaved you to the past and robbed you of the future, you must first confront that past without exception. This, by its very nature is no simple task, but one I believe that through due diligence, perseverance, and understanding is not insurmountable. It is most significant that one always remember and never forget: "it is not where you came from that is important but where you are going that matters." So, lest I leave you in a state of darkness and confusion, let me begin by giving you a brief history of myself that I hope you may find helpful on this novel journey of yours through paradise.

SENTIMENTS OF LOVE

I now wish to speak of love, and from the memories of my earliest childhood, how it was that I had experienced this unknown sentiment and most sacred emotion. It was by way of a gift, totally unexpected and least of all understood. I remember receiving this sacrament as a child, when I went upstairs and entered into my parents' bedroom to wake them up on Christmas day. I recall casting my eyes upon this big box sitting on the floor wrapped in Christmas paper with a bow attached to it. My parents instructed me to open it; within there was a little yellow pedal car, which I immediately pulled out from the box then joyfully began pedaling my way around the bedroom. It was the first gift of significance that I had ever received, and far exceeded my wildest dreams and expectations.

This is the earliest expression of love that I can recall dating back to my childhood days; least of all because of the little pedal car, but most treasured was the beautiful memory of my parents lying together in bed and being awakened by this intrusive little boy. It was the first time in my life that I had ever experienced such an immense feeling of tenderness and love, which I assumed would endure forever. However, as the years unfold and life dictates its inevitable change, we too must keep pace with it. If only I could have back that moment in time I would, above all else, choose to remain there forever cradled in love's memory and eternal embrace.

But things such as these are not meant to be. As time moves forward changing our lives to conform with it, so also does love evolve. What was once beloved and cherished above all else, must now give way to that which blossoms unto a greater love; not so much unlike the seasons that yield their essence in cycles, nor very different from those autumn leaves falling off the tree in winter, only to be replenished by the fresh new buds of spring.

NUANCES OF CHILDHOOD

There was a time in my childhood when I was educated in the narrow discipline of a religious institution. Rules mandated that boys not socialize with girls, and that even looking upon them in a curious way was somehow depicted as immoral and unholy. After about five years of this training and finding out that it was contrary to everything that was blossoming about me and burning within, I was persistent enough to persuade my parents to allow me to transfer into public school.

Life was quite different there, and I experienced such a sense of freedom that I would never have imagined could possibly exist. Then, shortly thereafter, there was to come this inevitable moment in time when my eyes fell upon this curious child in my class, who appeared to be the most beautiful girl that I had ever seen in my entire life. This was the very first time that I had ever felt such an indescribable warmth and polarizing attraction to someone of the opposite gender.

Well, as my curiosity broadened, I tried my best to make friends with this gorgeous child. I was battling an emotion that I did not understand and had never felt before. I would oftentimes look at her; when she caught me doing so, I would painstakingly force myself to break into a casual and sometimes awkward smile. This went on for a while, and we did shortly thereafter become somewhat distant friends; however, it soon became sadly clear to me that she did not share those same uncontrollable emotions that I had so passionately felt towards her. So, the lesson learned from this brief infatuation was: through her I came to understand that I was truly susceptible of an attraction to the opposite gender; however, I was not sure if there even existed a flip side to this proverbial coin.

As my first pursuit of interest in the opposite gender proved to be futile, I was left in a state of wonder and uncertainty. However, after having given up on this strange endeavor (that I would not have chosen had I any control over the matter), out of the blue something happened that was most astonishing and least of all anticipated. There was this very cute little girl in another class who seemed to take a curious interest in me, and it was the first time I had ever experienced anything like this. Although it was she who first initiated contact with me, it made little difference and shortly thereafter we became very special friends.

This child was so beautiful and loving that it soon became quite evident to me; she was the opposite side to that proverbial coin that I had once wondered even existed. Thereafter, for a short while we talked, walked to and from school, attended parties, and even danced together. In fact, she was the very first girl that I had ever kissed.

What happened to this relationship, though very straightforward, still requires a brief explanation so as to be understood in its entire context. I believe the short answer to this enigma to be: that her tender sentiments towards me far exceeded my shallow understanding of her. Although it pains me even unto this day to reflect back upon it, I would be remiss in not saying that never once did I ever take her love for granted. I cherished and respected her feelings and devotion more than one could ever imagine; I just think that discovering the other side of that proverbial coin in her was the end of the mission for me. So it came to pass, that after finally realizing this affection which had heretofore been so elusive sitting right there in the palm of my hand, I regretfully turned my back on it and we parted ways.

However, I believe it is worth mentioning one last episode of this friendship that will remain forever enshrined in my heart. I was invited to a party at her house by her older sister, who must have understood what she was going through after our separation. In an attempt to console her, she had set up this gathering as a last ditch effort to try and bring us back together again. Unbeknownst to me I accepted the invitation; though feeling a bit uncomfortable about the situation, I nonetheless found my way to her home.

I remember we were playing a game where a person would be blindfolded and the other gender would give this individual a kiss. The object of the game was to then guess who it was that kissed you. Anyway, as it turned out, it was my turn to be blindfolded and kissed. After that memorable embrace, never did I have any doubt whatsoever who it was that delivered that warm, heartfelt, bundle of emotion, which to this very day I shall never forget. As fate would have it, this was to be the last kiss that we ever shared together. What I regret most of all about this little romance is not that last kiss that we exchanged nor even the way we parted that evening (although at the time I could never have imagined how I would soon thereafter long for what once was), but why I chose to end such a relationship like this that could possibly have endured forever.

A SPECIAL PLACE IN TIME

I can look as far back in time as my memory has preserved for me and in doing so I remember the good as well as the bad. All of the good in my life came to me from others, while most of the bad was of my own doing. I wish I could turn back the hands of time and have another go around, but second chances are far and few; thus, it goes without saying, life is a phenomenon that only progresses towards the future. Such being the case, hindsight is always 20-20 and amounts to little more than wishful thinking and regret about what could or might have been. However, only this contrite, meager, consolation have I managed to accept and live with, notwithstanding the distraction of vain and unnecessary rationalization: I had my opportunities and for the most part squandered them.

Let me speak now of the good that was bestowed upon me from the inception of my existence. I had a loving family who nurtured me, caring adults who taught me, and friends whom I truly cherished. Unfortunately, despite all this, there seemed to be a void in me that remained unfulfilled. So, the search for that elusive something that might fill my emptiness, or someone who could understand my most deepest sentiments was, what I believe, the cause of so much of my grief.

Looking back, the good that I lived and breathed emanated from the aspirations and ideals that I sought. Just as man and woman were meant to be together so too are boy and girl. As this logic worked its way into my life; at an early age and after what seemed to be somewhat of a struggle, I found that first ray of sunshine incarnate in the gender of a female. We shortly thereafter became best friends; through her beauty, grace, and infinite smile, for the first time in my life I experienced the secret meaning of love hidden in a special someone who was an outsider and not a member of my immediate family.

Oh, how I remember that day and the way it changed my life forever: giving it new meaning, hope, and a prayer for the future. This was the good to which I have spoken; as it turned out, probably that of which I was not worthy. Yet, I was destined to find something unsettling in this relationship that I had never experienced before, which I was totally defenseless and unprepared to confront. Sadly, it was that common emotion which is prevalent among the most insecure of individuals and carries with it the scourge of the unforgiving.

It is only to you millennials that I wish to give this little piece of advice; it would amount to nothing more than old news to those who have come before you and have either survived or, like myself, fallen prey to this hideous monster. However, due to the pathetic and shameful characteristics that define this demon, I sincerely doubt that you will have ever heard before such a painful revelation as that of which I am about to confess.

Jealousy my friends (though only a human instinct) is such a destructive emotion that I would not wish it even upon my most mortal enemy (if I had one). Having felt and experienced that madness and realizing what it cost me at a time when life and love was so promising, I could not bear to witness another individual so helplessly possessed. For believe me my friends, this envious spirit is a real game changer; consequently, there is no way to fix it or send him back once that train has left the station.

If you would please indulge me for just a moment that I might give you a bit of counsel I would suggest only this: should you ever experience this devil sneaking upon you in the dark of night or at a moment when you least expect it, first and foremost, you must confront him with your head so that he does not find the path to your heart. For once in place, there is no easy way to rid yourself of this destructive demon until long after all the damage is done.

Having said this, it seems strange to me that upon looking back to that very special place in time, I must admit that there was absolutely no rhyme or reason whatsoever for me to have become so jealous and enraged that fateful evening. My emotions got the best of me at a time when I had least expected it, and I was helpless to fend off this demon and save myself from all that was to follow. This jealous rage that had so unexpectedly overcome me served not only to fan the flames of my own self destruction, but most importantly caused irreparable harm and unforgiving embarrassment to the one girl that I had truly loved.

This jealous devil found the path of no resistance to my heart, and as a consequence thereof proved to be fatal. What the loss of that very beautiful child (at such a special place in time) would take from me was just the tip of the iceberg of what was yet to come. It was the beginning of a lonely journey that would send me tumbling into the depths of chaos and confusion, and for a very long time not even the hand of mercy could reach me to extend its forgiveness.

As I reminisce one last time about all the good this girl had shown me, I must also express what an honor it was to know that she once cared; however, I will always remember and shall never forget the tragic event which had caused my fateful undoing that memorable night. But my philosophy has always been to look at the sunny side of things and try to make the very best out of a bad situation. Let me close by simply stating: this short lived relationship was very tender, extremely loving, and conceived at a very special place in time where both sides of that proverbial coin complement each other and ultimately become one.

THE ESSENCE OF ADOLESCENCE

Just as the night turns into day, days into weeks, weeks into months, and months into years, so also at the time of conception an infant is formed. At the time of birth, it will inevitably evolve on its journey through infancy, childhood, adolescence, and manhood. I would like now to speak of adolescence.

What is the essence of adolescence: is it the outgrowth of childhood or the maturation of the child? At first blush, the question appears to present a distinction without a difference; nonetheless, there is a subtle difference. For as to the former, it would appear not so unlike that of the snake who sheds its old skin periodically. However, with regard to the latter, it is the transformation from one state of being into another.

As a youth, again I first understood the meaning of adolescence in the persona of a female. Strange that each stage of the life of a man should be configured by the opposite gender, but I do not make the rules. Let me begin by saying that it was, as best as I can remember, a cold and melancholy winter day somewhere back in time when I laid my eyes on what appeared to be that of an angel; something of such beauty that only myths can describe. After this treasured and unforgettable moment, I just knew that somehow we would be inextricably bound together in this life forever.

I immediately began to pursue this sentiment: whether it was simply to understand and unravel the hidden mystery behind it, or to find out why it presented itself to me as and when it did I cannot say. But just as all treasures in life are not attainable without a bit of a struggle, this also was not to be an easy task. I toiled, I strived, and I failed. Then something which I least expected happened! I succeeded. From that moment on the essence of my early adolescence was forged.

Yes, adolescence was a great place in time. Life again was meaningful, and I began to care deeply once more about someone outside of the immediate family. This beautiful individual was now not only in my life, but also in my dreams and never out of my thoughts and prayers. I remember each and every part of the day we spent together, and nothing could ever please me more than just being with her.

However, as fate would have it, I again made some bad choices. What I did was to put country before this earthly angel (because at the time it seemed like a good idea), so we parted and I went on my way alone. Nevertheless, she waited years for my return; although I did return, it was not as that same adolescent who had left her behind so long ago, but rather a lost soul suspended somewhere between the skeleton of youth and the shadow of man. This was the irreconcilable difference between us: I was no longer the adolescent that she once knew, and still not the man that she had hoped for. Would that I could have somehow bridged that gap I would gladly have done so in a heartbeat. For believe me, she was well worth the effort and deserving of much more than one could ever imagine.

Nonetheless, we desperately tried to pick up the pieces of the past and resume a life which, by all appearances, would seem to have been preordained. A relationship, that from the very first moment I looked into those beautiful blue eyes I believed would be inseparable and everlasting. However, no matter how much one tries and despite everything that she was willing to sacrifice for me, it was still not enough. You see, notwithstanding the love and adoration that I truly felt towards her: when a man is so vain that he sincerely believes the world has set aside a special place of glory for him, a kingdom where only he is welcome; then his folly is not just selfish disillusionment, but in truth amounts to nothing more than a person so full of himself that he has lost all perspective of reality. Unfortunately, so it was with me.

As I look back in time, I still remember the last evening we spent together as if it were yesterday; with tears rolling down her cheeks and sadness in my heart, I made it clear to her that I was on a mission and that she could not be a part of it. Now it came to pass, that shortly thereafter when my mission had failed (or reality had set in), I would only then begin to experience remorse for the pain and suffering that I caused her and the magnitude of the loss which I had brought upon myself. As you probably already know: "timing is everything," and unfortunately for me it was just too late to do anything about it. Such being the case, you shall soon learn that there is much truth in that aged old maxim: "what goes around comes around."

As I stated earlier: "strange that each stage of the life of a man should be configured by the opposite gender," but I do not make the rules. However, having said this, I sincerely believe that we do have a say in what the end result of our lives will be. For life, metaphorically speaking, is somewhat like a game of chess wherein the players move about pieces on the board in anticipation of what the other might do, but always with only one objective in mind: to capture the opponent's king. So, when confronted with the unexpected one must always improvise, then make a choice about which piece he is willing to sacrifice in order to save his king.

I would like believe that although I may have made the wrong moves, everything that I had surrendered in the process to save my king was really to protect my queen. However, this would only amount to wishful thinking. What I did was of my own choosing and driven by nothing more than selfish indifference; accordingly, I must now accept and live with the consequences. Let me close by simply stating that this relationship was truly the best thing that could of ever happened to me in my youth. One that I shall always cherish, never forget, and for which I will forever remain eternally grateful.

THE EVOLUTION OF MAN

We come as children, grow into adolescence, and evolve as man. So have we always been taught. But there remains a stage in this transition into man that has been overlooked, which lies in the gap that spans the bridge between adolescence and man. For man comes into being not as the direct offshoot of adolescence, but from the outgrowth of adolescence and maturity into man. This period of incubation is not fixed by age or time; it is defined only by the achievements and conquests of the individual. For where adolescence has run its course, there the chaotic period has its beginning. It is in this phase of constant change that chaos persists, until through self-overcoming the transition from adolescence to man is realized.

Just what is a man? one might ask. I too have pondered this riddle and have not yet been able to solve it. It is my most fervent hope that short of answering this question I might, at least, give you a glimpse into a dream and vision that I once had, which I believe might help you to crack this nut.

A long time ago I was lost in the jungle. I was alone and had no one to talk to or confide in who could help me extricate myself from that lonely place. The days were seemingly far too short and the nights way too long. I had only the animals that I had encountered to speak with; although they seemed to understand me, yet they could give me no guidance.

It was not so bad at first, but after a while I felt hopelessly lost and came to the bitter conclusion that I would never find my way home. I walked and searched, looking here and there, seeking to find clear passage from the thick brush and canopy. If only I could find uninterrupted daylight, I kept thinking, that would at least point me in the right direction. But this was not to be. I walked day and night through the heat of summer and the cold of winter. My feet grew callous and my body weary. As this night was to be no different from all of the others, it was the usual time when exhaustion had set in and I could march no further that I decided to retire for the evening.

As I began looking for a place where I might shelter myself from the elements, I remember finding a monument in that jungle standing alone amidst all the trees and shrubs. Since darkness was quickly descending, I decided to accept the invitation to sit and rest upon that solitary stone then fell into a deep sleep. It was during this time that I had dreamed of a place way back many years ago where, as a very young boy, I used to go and sit by a stream that flowed in a little creek along-side the railroad tracks. It was just a place where I could sit and forget, for the time being, what might have been on my mind that day; whether it be loneliness, school work, or anything else that would take me away from the peace and serenity of that little stream.

Although, every now and then one's worst nightmare (even during the best of times) is waking up from a peaceful dream, that was not to be the situation here. When I had opened my eyes, I experienced something that was so very strange and at the same time inexplicably delightful. A vision which had filled me with so much wonder and surprise, that I have not yet found the words to adequately describe such a feeling of elation and gratitude.

After I had awaken, lo and behold, there was no more jungle and I found myself in a cemetery sitting on the very stone where my paternal grandparents were interred, many years ago, when I was just a small child. Filled with joy I pinched myself to see if I was dreaming, and I was not; this cannot be I thought! If this is not a dream, then how did I get here? What about being hopelessly lost in the jungle, was I dreaming then? One or the other most assuredly had to be a dream, because how can you be in two different places at the same time I queried.

Well, as I pondered this situation, I began to wonder if I had ever been lost in the jungle before; then it came to me that I had, once not so far in the distant past. Just as that experience was definitely not a dream neither was this. You see, I did in fact spend the night in the cemetery on the stone of my beloved grandparents, and so one could at least argue that much is true. Taking this one step further I could, in theory, have been in two different places at the same time if, but only if, I had never fully extricated myself from that dreadful jungle not so long ago.

However, something then happened that was to change my life forever. It was just at the break of dawn, when darkness was no more, that from out of the shadows there emerged a silhouette which appeared to me to be that of a man. But just as quickly as this phantom came in that timeless moment, it vanished in an instant; leaving me no means by which to learn of its identity. What was it that caused this dream and vision that evening which I remember so long ago? Well, to answer this question I must begin with a little preface. As I said earlier, at that point in time I was suspended somewhere between the "skeleton of youth and the shadow of man"; I was hopelessly lost in the jungle and unable to find my way.

It was, as I remember back then, the radiant smile of a most beautiful and gracious woman which had so permeated the innermost fibers of being that I had lost total control of the moment; my heart broke out from within my chest, then like a little bird that had fallen from its nest and trembling in fear found solace in the palm of my hand. Because this tender heart of mine wanted nothing more than to be loved and caressed, it was eagerly willing to accept whatever the future had in store for it. After I managed to put my heart back into its rightful place, I decided to follow whatever path it was destined to lead me. As I reluctantly did so, it was only conditioned upon the sincere hope that whatever it most fervently desired would serve to rescue me from a confused and broken past.

For how else could it be? Once there was a little girl who adored me that I turned my back on, only because through her sincerity and simplicity I was shown the flip side of that proverbial coin that I did not know even existed; then a childhood friend that truly cared and had given me so much, who I had nonetheless frightened away forever by exposing to her first hand the dark side of my jealous rage; finally, an adolescent angel that I had pushed aside for fear that she might intrude upon a kingdom that I had envisioned only for myself, whose true love and unwavering devotion was no match when pitted against my stubborn vanity and foolish sense of grandiosity.

Now, after all this, there comes into my life such a divine woman who was all I could have ever hoped for; it goes without saying, one that I was determined to pursue until the end of time if necessary. It was through her that I sought redemption from the past, and hoped to erase the scars from all those self-inflicted wounds; I was prepared to do everything in my power and give whatever was required, in order to win that elusive prize that had so many times been in my grasps, yet somehow managed to slip away. But, as you shall soon discover, this was not to be. For the first time in my life; having experienced such a sense of total rejection, did it finally descend upon me what it must have felt like to those others of long ago whom I had disappointed and let down in one way or another.

Nevertheless, I did faithfully obey my heart's command, even though I somehow knew in the back of my mind that there was not to be a golden pot at the end of this rainbow. Alas, my friends, this ill fated romance which I had once memorialized "the first living breath of my silent longing" was short lived. As fate would have it, she had about as much interest in me as one might anticipate when about to greet a leper for the first time. The realization of this came to me as no small surprise; I felt truly betrayed by that same heart which I had nourished and comforted from the very first moment that it laid in my hand, pulsating like a premature organism not yet ready for the world that awaits it.

However, it was not this great disappointment in life that I regret so much, but rather the infinite depths of depression and despair to which it drove me. Though there was no excuse for it, I nonetheless fault myself for having so unwittingly succumbed to it. As it did seem to me to be the end of the world as I had known it then, would that there was any way to finish it I would have gladly submitted. Yet, despite all that, at long last did I finally come to terms with this bittersweet illusion. Only after much reflection was I able to comfort myself with the simple truth: even though her love and devotion lie in the arms of another, the memory of her and that radiant smile shall forever remain here beside me.

After many years of chasing the dragon and the passing of a few more relationships that were too insignificant to mention, I finally came to the realization of a simple maxim that stays with me even unto this day: “it is not how much you are loved in this life that is of any significance; only the ability and power to love unconditionally is all that really matters.” Now, is not love synonymous with the true essence of a man? It begins with the joy of the moment as the transformation from adolescence seems but a dream, then loses itself in an instant when (unaware and unprepared) it begins its journey down that long and winding road the that lies ahead.

THE PATH TO REDEMPTION

So, the time of reckoning was upon me and I was left with only two choices. I could take option number one: accept my ill fate and go down that road to a place where I had been before which leads to nowhere (and believe me you don't want to go there). Or, I could choose option number two: pick up the pieces, gather them unto myself, and move on. The choice, though seemingly an easy one, is not so cut and dry. You see, *quitting* in an alphabetical order comes before *success*. The one who quits is at least guaranteed the consequences of his choice, whereas the other who chooses to carry onward will have no such assurances. Well, it should seem as no surprise to you what choice I made; I took the way that leads to a place not yet in existence, that treacherous path of redemption where the only guarantees and assurances lie in the moment itself.

Left for dead by my own hand I desperately felt the need to live on. After all, life had always been good to me, and it would seem only fair and equitable that I should at least entrust myself to it just one more time. Though broken and humiliated I somehow found the courage to return home once again; if only to find solace in those compassionate souls of the past who had cared so deeply for me, yet despite myself loved me nonetheless.

This shelter and eternal love that had never once abandoned me was still not enough to heal my wounds. Although they tried desperately to fill the void that was in me, this effort was just not to be. It was only my vanity, stubbornness, and hope that propelled me forward, and I soon found myself on the road again. Broken hearted, in tears, and feeling neglected, is how I left behind for the last time those who loved me so dearly and had given all that they had.

Moving forward down that chosen path not knowing where it was leading, and comforted only by my sorrow I pressed onward nonetheless. However, this time was to be different from all the others. There would be no family or friends to fall back upon when the times got tough. I was alone again; far across the landscape from where I left behind those who truly loved me, and I had nothing more than just a sliver of hope and dream of success to guide the way. Yes, it was the vision of a better tomorrow that led each step of my journey and allowed me to sleep at night as best I could. But oftentimes it appeared as though I was just kidding myself, pretending that somehow something good lie in store for me.

You see, each day brought nothing new and often seemed as if it never would. But then I looked upon the most beautiful woman that I had ever seen. Plain and simple was she, and all that I once again could have ever hoped for. This was the one individual that I somehow knew from the moment when I first laid my eyes on her, that I wanted to spend the rest of my life with. A short while later and to my great surprise something truly marvelous happened. This wonderful woman first accepted my promise to love and cherish her for the rest of my life, then opened wide her benevolent arms to embrace what very little I had to offer.

Thereafter, she bore me two beautiful sons that changed my life forever, and for which I will always remain eternally grateful. So, from the abysmal depths of misery and despair I had risen to the infinite heights of joy and contentment; through her love and all that she had given me, was I thus able to find that elusive peace of mind that I had so desperately been searching for.

PART II

THE AWAKENING

So it was, that after forty five years and the passing of a new millennium, I had awakened from a deep sleep only to find that all things patiently await their time of becoming. It was then that I first asked myself this: why must a man wait so long and bear such a heavy burden, before the essence of his existence finds true meaning? I answered that question as follows: what purpose would man serve here on earth if all being were not a mystery, and life itself only a puzzle with which he is destined to shape the future from the pieces of his past?

Then, with the breaking of dawn, there came to me a new sunrise which poured its radiant light upon all that was and all that is yet to come. What has been since the cradle and shall be unto the grave is but a moment in time; it is man's desire of fulfillment, forged from experience and cast in hope. Somewhere suspended between the past and the future his fate hangs in the balance; while destiny guides him, he continues to search the universe in the hope of discovering the meaning of his existence. From this endless pursuit and quest of the unknown (through trial and error) he seeks to find the answer to that aged old question: "who am I, and why am

I here?"

What would our lives be were it otherwise? Is not the desire for truth absolutely necessary if one is to achieve peace of mind? Who among us can find that tranquility within ourselves, when refusing to accept the truth is tantamount to living a life of fantasy and disillusionment? Though as painful as the truth may sometimes be; is it not more courageous to challenge it head on for what it is, as opposed to taking refuge in the belly of the lie? So, I would now ask you this: is it not much wiser to embrace the heartbreak, whatever it may be, than to fear the humiliation? For believe me my friends, even a broken heart may mend itself in time; however, there is much less hope for the redemption of a submissive and humiliated spirit.

Therefore, fear not the truth my friends, for it will comfort you in your time of need and can only serve to make you stronger. Embrace it with open arms as your fate in life, even though it may lead you to what would prove to be the most devastating and painful experience that you have ever encountered. Always remember, by accepting the truth for what it is, you will honor that which in you is your greatest virtue: *honesty*. Thus, avoid falsehood at all costs whether it be by words or deeds. For lies rolling off the tongue or guile gesticulating from the extremities are but one and the same thing: *deception*. Lastly, (and most importantly) never be hypocritical under any circumstances whatsoever. Even though hypocrisy is the quickest way to self-aggrandizement, it is also the mirror image of vanity and a bottom feeder of all mankind. Such being the case, who amongst us can predict when these hypocrites will ever tire of themselves and be satisfied with that which they consume?

HUMANITY

To love and appreciate the earth and all its inhabitants is essential to an understanding of the miracle of life. But to many the earth is but a sponge, with which to squeeze to the very last drop all of her natural resources in order to amass enormous wealth. It is through this process of self-enrichment that humanity and all other living things are considered nothing more than a mere impediment; consequently, destruction of the earth and its species is dismissed with a wave of the hand under the self-serving doctrine of necessity and collateral damage.

Beginning from the earliest time when man first arrived and left his footprint here on this earth, he has always deemed himself superior to all other species and supreme ruler of the planet. In the pursuit of material wealth has he set out to destroy whatever stands in his way, and conquer all that resists him. However, even as the earth shall one day become too small for man's ambitions, so also will the seeds of his greed blossom and ripen into the fruit of his own self-destruction.

For things must not continue as they are today, in such a manner that the planet cannot keep pace with this incessant bombardment, depletion, and destruction of its natural resources. The earth's deep strata is weakening due to the drilling and fracking for oil and natural gas; the tropical rain forests are being rapidly depleted by the ambitions of the logging industry; even the very air that we breathe is grossly contaminated by energy emissions and other pollutants; all of which have caused deleterious effects to the earth, its inhabitants, and the atmosphere.

These are but a few of the many things that threaten the longevity of this planet which we must seriously consider and remedy. Do I advocate the cessation of all these activities which are necessary to our daily lives today as we know them to be? Absolutely not! However, what I do humbly suggest is: that in the pursuit of these industrial endeavors we proceed with reasonable caution and maintain production to a moderate degree, such that the end result of these practices will not eviscerate the planet nor cause further harm to the earth and her species. Alas, the time is at hand; it is therefor incumbent upon each and every one of us to act with prudence, so that there might still be a place left for future generations to flourish and prosper.

BRAVE HUNTERS

It was during the Neanderthal period when the primitive form of man first evolved, that he hunted beasts and other prey as food to appease his hunger and skins to cover his nakedness. This sacrifice of life to sustain life was then, as it is today, considered innocent and necessary to man's survival and comfort. But what of the cowardly who deem themselves brave, and while armed and dangerous stalk and kill their innocent targets for sport?

To such as these, there is no redemption so long as they continue in their senseless and vile crimes against nature. The hunters of today shall be the hunted of tomorrow. While their weapons are cocked and finger on the trigger, so too is the bow of life bent in the steady hand of the archer; with a fixed eye he shall let go his arrows which shall strike at the very heart of these brave hunters, and they too shall perish.

Even though there is much to be forgiven due to the needs and ancestral practices of our predecessors, this persistent ignorance that you call sport is unacceptable. You have shed much innocent blood and caused irreparable harm thereby. In your folly, you have threatened extinction of the species and have plundered the earth of her lineage.

Man, who was born with so much common sense and bestowed the inalienable gift of intelligence; chosen as the descendants and caretakers of the earth has somehow lost his way, and shall not find himself until this despicable conduct is no more.

You created a dreadful sport out of the sanctity of life itself you brave hunters, and have devastated the earth in the process. But the time is near when the hunter shall be the hunted, and you shall find no solace to shelter yourselves from the consequences of your heinous deeds. For the earth shall one day abandon you, even as you have forsaken her. Heretofore, let there be no more killing other than to appease hunger, and prevent imminent danger to life and property.

THE BODY POLITIC

The great wealth which the few possess has become the will that governs the masses. With this wealth and power, these resourceful few would bend and shape the spirit of the masses into a tool that is suitable only to their own needs and desires. It is to this end where corruption and power have its genesis, and are enshrined as the embodiment of that which is today called politics. But believe me my friends, where the political body has its roots there the spirit ceases to be free. For how can the spirit be free when it is controlled by that very force that imprisons it?

Always have we been told by the few and powerful of that which is good and in our best interest; however, that which is truly good and in our best interest, is oftentimes in sharp contrast with the mores and dictates of the uninformed few who have imposed their will upon us. They have deemed criminal such things as the recreational use of natural herbs and other innocuous behavior, while at the same time immunizing the alcohol manufactures and tobacco growers. Their integrity has been further compromised by the lobbyist; who persuade them into promoting such entities as the pharmaceutical industry, and approving the issuance of patents for drugs prescribed for almost every ailment under the sun (whether real or imagined).

What their mores and politics dictate is not only inconsistent with the innate good with which we are all endowed, but also contrived from an uninformed, inherently biased rationalization which flies in the face of common sense, and is at odds with everything that a free and intelligent spirit stands for.

Henceforth, we must no longer allow these archaic beliefs and irrational policies that have heretofore been heaped upon us under the auspices of the body politic, to either dictate the breadth of our morality or calibrate the scope of our birthright. Rather, we must continuously strive to relegate the politics of the day into that which it really is: an embarrassment of the past. Then, as we seek to plant the seed of a new hope for tomorrow, let us make it our goal and sole objective to rescue from that shameful past a future that is filled with promise; built upon the foundation of fairness and the concepts of equality and justice for all.

POLITICIANS

Some enter the profession of politics with the very best of intentions, while others seek the political arena only as a means to further their own self-interests. They enter office and swear an oath to uphold and defend. Yet, once in office, they abuse the public trust and betray their oath, solely to appease the "special interests" of those powers that be who have financed their candidacy. They delight very much in saying things like, "by the people and for the people" or "liberty and justice for all"; however, to them this is mere poppycock, and their deeds reflect only that these speeches are hollow and not grounded in the will of the people.

When one cannot say what he truly thinks nor do what he sincerely believes, then his words are vain and his posture meaningless. In truth, these historical concepts envisioned by our forefathers with the intent that they serve the needs of the people have all but vanished over time; consequently, the last remnants of those constitutional guarantees (that idealistically remain intact) have been eroded to such an extent, that to raise them is to do little more than exalt form over substance.

When these elected officials speak of those ideals which the founders considered to be the inalienable rights of all Americans, it always amounts to little more than noble monologues which have been sacrificed in furtherance of the objectives and goals of the wealthy and privileged. The politicians of today are bought and paid for; they are merely puppets in the hands of the powerful few, whose sole mission here on earth is to enrich themselves off the backs of the many.

Yet, these politicians have the audacity to present themselves as servants of the people when, in truth, they serve only themselves and the rich and powerful to whom they are beholden. But there shall come a time when they too will answer for what they have done, and the truth of their betrayal will stand revealed before the face of the sun. At that lonely hour, neither their self-pity nor remorse will suffice to ease the conscience and rescue them from their own shame and despair.

GOVERNMENT

Government is the offspring and image of the body politic drafted in its likeness by the politicians. Always have we been told that government is synonymous with "the will of the people," but this is only half the truth. To be sure, in a democratic republic the government is idealized as "the will of the people"; however, in reality, it is the ambitions of the powerful few that impose their will upon the many, and call this imbalance of power "the will of the people."

Would that it were otherwise, and "the will of the people" was the check and balance of the embodiment and power of government; thus, as a consequence thereof, the government would serve only "the will of the people." However, if history has shown us anything at all it has demonstrated at least one thing for sure: "that might makes right." It follows: that when the words of the less prosperous are silenced by the power of the wealthy few, then there can never be any semblance of a government that is "by and for the people."

But there shall come a time when the people will tire of living under such an inequitable balance of power and demand change; accordingly, in a democratic society, as a matter of public policy money will be taken out of the equation and no longer control the outcome of elections or the direction of the future. Though these things are not yet to be, they shall one day prove to be more than just a mere afterthought. For even as the seasons cannot hasten their becoming, so also must change patiently await its time. Hence, the time for change is inevitably upon us.

HEALTH AND WELFARE

The government has always dictated what is and is not good for the health and welfare of the people. That which is forbidden as not good is often codified as a crime, and carries with it a penalty. However, that which is accepted as good is enshrined as the health and welfare of the people, and oftentimes carries with it a profit and source of great wealth. There have been times when what was considered good later became not good, only to be deemed good again when it was profitable to make it so.

Even today there are products that have been classified as health hazards, yet they remain in the stream of commerce and are taxed as a source of revenue. In truth, to ban these goods in an effort to promote the health and welfare of the people is a double edged sword. First, it would halt the cash flow of the producers and manufacturers of these commodities, and thus sever the purse strings of the government from its source. Secondly, there would no longer be any trickle down economic effect of the profits from these intangibles (in the form of campaign contributions) which ultimately find their way into the pocketbooks and wallets of the unscrupulous politicians.

Throughout history, we have been shown that even from the early days of prohibition to the current times of the legalization of prostitution and some recreational drugs; when the government is helpless to stop the prohibited trade or practice it will turn around and legalize it, then under the auspices of its taxation powers collect a tariff. Just take for example the business of gambling, wherein those innovative entrepreneurs of the past risked their personal liberty and capital in the underground numbers game (today's lottery), or accepted wagers on professional sports betting and card games (today's casinos) when it was unlawful to do so.

Please tell me my friends: what is it that has legitimized these criminal statutes of the past? if not the questionable policy and practice of government and the states to look the other way and show a bit more tolerance, whenever it can find some justification to levy a tax on a product or service that it is helpless to prohibit. In theory, one might conclude that we now live in a somewhat more civilized and common sense society; accordingly, that which was once forbidden and considered illicit has now been sanitized for the greater good.

However, the truth of the matter is: that it is no longer a question of whether or not the banning of these harmless vices are considered to be in the best interest of the health and safety of the people. On the contrary, what we have today is a self-serving doctrine of convenience which is realized from this one basic rationalization: when it is expedient for the government to act in *its* best interest and collect a share of the profits wherever it can, then the ensuing logic that follows always seems to be *what is the harm in that?*

JUSTICE

Justice is a noble concept but it is not reality. We pride ourselves in that aged old maxim: "and liberty and justice for all." But history has repeatedly shown that justice is reserved only to those who can afford it. Once it was just to enslave a people and transport them from their motherland to toil and labor in this land. Today, those who wish to leave their homelands to seek an honest wage in this land are frowned upon, and even considered criminals.

Always have we sought to have it both ways when it served our needs and interests to do so. When it was once considered appropriate to import slave labor for a fee, it was looked upon as merely a necessary evil so that the wealthy landowners could thrive and profit off the backs of these slaves (oftentimes scarred by the inhumane imposition of the whip). So too were immigrants from other lands once welcomed into this land, simply because their cheap labor served our nation's economy and was an efficient and indispensable means of building the country.

But things have changed, some for the better and others for the worse. As for the better, after much resistance and a bloody civil war which divided the nation; those brave patriots on the side of equality and freedom, following the dictates of their conscience and a sense of justice, had given all they had to make it possible that these practices of involuntary servitude were at long last put to rest. Forever has it been throughout our nation's history, that men such as these who are asked to put their lives on the line for the greater good of the country have always answered the call.

However, as to those patriots who served on the losing side of history, they too were nonetheless patriots in their own right. It was for a cause that their fathers and grandfathers professed was reasonable and necessary, that they were noble enough to accept the challenge and willing to sacrifice their lives for the sake of these ingrained beliefs. It has always been the case throughout history and even unto this very day; those who have little to gain but everything to lose, are inevitably sacrificed to benefit and enhance the status and interests of the wealthy and prominent few.

As to the other dark side of our nation's history; long after the railroad tracks, bridges, subways, and other infrastructure had been erected and put in place by the toil and sweat of immigrants, today's foreign laborers who come to this land to seek an honest wage are ridiculed and bemoaned as somehow less dignified. Yet, despite this lament and outrage of what is denounced as an immigrant invasion into this country (mostly by the uninformed who dwell far from these borders and are not impacted thereby), it is hard to imagine how they have somehow forgotten who it is that cultivates those fields and picks the fruits and vegetables that are placed upon their tables.

Lastly, so as to not add insult to injury, let us not forget that we ourselves who came as foreigners to this land and planted our flag, stole and plundered all that there was from the indigenous people. *We came, we saw, and we conquered,* this much is true. Always has it been taught us that there was virtue in this. That our conquests were achieved by the hand of the almighty and ordained through the grace of God. But shameless is that virtue and boundless its hypocrisy. Though it is true "that we are not responsible for the sins of our fathers," yet honesty still demands that we must at least be honorable enough to acknowledge them. However, we refuse even to do this. It is much more convenient to dismiss it with a wave of the hand, and excuse ourselves by simply saying: the slaughter of the indigenous people who refused to peacefully surrender their freedom was inevitable, and that slavery was just something brought over here by our ancestors which we inherited from the Europeans.

But the time will come when even our opulence will not suffice to countenance such guilt and shame. That very arrogance which is now eroding beneath the weight and burden of unjust wars. Unjust and unnecessary wars that sacrifice the sanctity of human life, and costs the government unspeakable amounts in treasure. These unjust and inhumane wars, trumped up by the propaganda of the unscrupulous politicians solely to benefit the rich and powerful.

OF TRIBUNALS

We have put in place tribunals to uphold the laws of the land and mete out justice. I myself, a true believer in justice, have little faith in the tribunals of today. Although set up to practice in the wisdom of Solomon, they have proved to be little more than a conglomerate of political hacks involved in the practice of politics and not justice.

There was a time when those appointed to the bench not only were loyal to their oath to uphold the law, but did in fact mete out justice. However, the time has long passed since the nobility of these tribunals have maintained their independence. The jurists of today have sadly betrayed their oaths in pursuit of political agenda. You laugh and shake your heads in disbelief at these words, but the time will come when you too will stand in judgment. On that day, may justice be more merciful to you than you have been towards it.

You have sworn an oath to uphold the laws of the land so that justice might be served, but you have failed miserably in this endeavor. If these be harsh words, so be it. Judges and Justices who have served their office with honor and the utmost integrity should not be offended, as I do not speak to them. In fact, I have had the privilege of knowing many of these noble jurists who, in the face of ridicule and public outrage have followed their conscience nonetheless; hence, when left with the choice between justice and scorn, have always demonstrated that rare courage to stand up and do the right thing.

However, these great men and women of the bench are few and in between; although their legacy will probably not survive them, what they have contributed to the profession will live on. For they are the role models of the future, and have set the standard of what every young judge should ascribe to. However, to those of you who conceal yourselves beneath your soiled robes, and masquerade around as arbiters of truth and justice I make no apologies. For you are but relics of the past soon to be retired and forgotten.

LAW ENFORCEMENT

This arm of the executive office enforces the law as written by the legislative branch of our tripartite system of government. In short, what I am referring to here is commonly called the police power. Law enforcement is necessary to the public's health and safety of its people. But all too often it falls far short of this noble endeavor. Oftentimes, instead of upholding its symbolism and sacred oath as peace keeper and protector of society, the badge is transformed into a sword which (under color of law) is wielded by some with impunity as an instrument of brutality.

The vast majority of peace officers execute their duties with professionalism and integrity, but all too many abuse this great power which has been vested in them. It is a dangerous dilemma we are confronted with when it comes to the recruitment and staffing of peace officers. On the one hand, it is necessary to fill the ranks sufficiently to serve the public trust; on the other, the standards required must be relaxed in order to meet this pressing challenge in an efficient manner.

I do not presume to have the solution to this conundrum; however, I would propose a process by which the proven failures of the past might be remedied in the future. Through intensive training must we educate these current and prospective peace officers about the history of our great nation, and define specifically what their roles are in protecting society and serving the advancement of all humanity. Having said this, I do not wish to sound naive. It is common knowledge that a peace officer has a very dangerous job and tremendous responsibility not only to the public, but most importantly to himself; to this end he must always try his best to do his work efficiently, cautiously, and with due care, such that at the end of the shift he can return home safely to his family.

I would first instill in them the solemn dedication to ascertain under all circumstances (consistent with their oath), that their duties be limited only to assist and protect the people they serve; to defend the government against all enemies foreign and domestic; and to uphold the laws of the land and the Constitution of the United States of America.

Thus, having been duly sworn and armed not only with a revolver or shielded by a badge, will these future peace officers be equipped with the knowledge, training, and understanding, that the job they do is more important and much greater than the power that is vested in them by virtue of their profession. Their credo shall be that life goes not backwards towards the dark ages (which is still all too prevalent amongst our leaders, politicians, and judges), but forward towards a brighter and better future for this country and the children of tomorrow for whom they shine.

REINVENTING THE WHEEL

Many things come to us in our lives of which we have little or no control. Some the good and others the less desirable. It is these less desirable things that we must find the courage and will to overcome. Where does one find the strength necessary to overcome the undesirable and thereby reinvent himself?

It is in the power of the creative self where one must go if he is to effect change. Deep down into this well of the unknown lies a reservoir of power which is the creative self. It has been there since the beginning of time and silently reposes in all of us. So it is, that we who were all conceived in it will be, from the inception of our birth, ultimately defined by it. You see, the creative self is a living organism which dictates our daily lives commensurate with the time and effort we devote to it. One can spend little or no time exploring this, and his understanding of himself, or lack thereof, will only mirror the image and opinions of how others conceive him to be.

However, if one is bold and courageous enough, he will seek to find the true essence of his being through exploration of this creative self. Oftentimes, it will come to him unconsciously in a dream when he is otherwise incapable of rational thinking. But dreams are, at best, as we know them to be: the pursuit of one's highest hope or the escape from one's deepest fear; something that is either fervently longed for or cautiously avoided.

Thus, even as in the dream where it takes the creative self to overcome the unconscious self, and thereby give that brief period of peace to the body and mind that it so desperately needs; so also must it be in our daily lives where it takes the creative self to overcome the conscience self, and in so doing yield that measure of knowledge and understanding which will direct the course of the future and shape the scope of our behavior consistent therewith.

True it is that man fears what he does not know. However, this fear of the unknown is not caused by ignorance of the unknown; it is the result of fear fixed in itself. When this fear is no more, the creative self reconfigures the body and mind and through this metamorphosis comes change. Once one is able to recognize this, then he is free to seek the creative self as a matter of right and without apprehension of what might lie in a vacuum. All these things are now known to him, and since knowledge is the precursor of wisdom the wheel of invention turns.

PART III

THE NEW MILLENNIUM

Every thousand years equals a millennium. Not everyone is fortunate enough to live to see one; some are just born at the wrong time, while others simply die before their time. But to those of us who have been lucky enough to have inherited this new millennium comes with it the responsibility to leave it in a better condition than we found it. Therefore, it is my intention to share with you some of the things I have thought about over the years, which I hope you will take notice; whether you agree or disagree, it is nonetheless my most fervent wish that you might find them helpful.

Looking back to the 20th century when I was born is bitter sweet. The joys of childhood, the pain of adolescence, and the responsibility of manhood. These are some of the emotions that I have experienced throughout my life that you too my children will soon discover. This unquenchable thirst for life that has consumed me from the inception of my birth, and that inescapable fear of death which still haunts me even unto this day are but a moment in time. As I look back with tenderness and gratitude upon this fledgling nation that I love, I still cannot forget the past and the pain of its social injustice that I loathed. Yet, all these things which have encompassed the first fifty years of my life are but a mere page of history, torn from that old millennial book of the last century.

It is for the children of tomorrow that I wish to forge a new piece of history, that they might hopefully look back upon someday with a sense of pride and without regret. Though one cannot turn back the hands of time and erase what once was; it is still not too late to reform the past and shape the future. Though my time here in this new millennium is limited, and quickly fading away like the sun that sets behind the mountains in the evening; it is my most fervent hope that, at the very least, I can try to make it a better place for these new millennials who must spend the rest of their lives in this 21st century.

In order that the best-interest of these children of the future might be served we must set aside our differences for the moment. For surely, would *not* a parent who loves his children sacrifice all that he has for them? He who would do otherwise knows not love, but only greed and selfish indifference. It is no secret that I too must regretfully admit that there was a time when I knew nothing of giving, and was only content to be on the receiving end of things. But, as I have painfully described above, in the end it was I alone who was left to pay the ultimate price for my misdeeds.

So let us always remember, "that love of our children's future is the only redemption from the past." Forget not, that those of you who have sown the seeds of discord amongst your fellow man have accomplished nothing more than the division of a nation. Though sad as this may be: you instigators and rabble rousers of today, who delight in race bating and steering up bigotry amongst men have learned nothing from the lessons of history. Even though it may appease your hatred to spout this nonsense, it pleases me even more to know that it is only you and your ilk that take comfort in such abominations.

"One nation under god" was the solemn oath of our forefathers, but in your sanctimonious arrogance have you succeeded only in eviscerating even this last hope. Though the bloodshed of this nation was the ink with which these bold words were once inscribed; it makes little difference today that we have erased them, and in their place have set forth policy and practice that obliterates and undermines even these very basic concepts of fairness and equality. Would that it were otherwise, and only those who have forsaken all that they have been entrusted with would suffer the consequences of their misdeeds; however, even this burden have they laid upon the backs of the children of this new millennium to bear.

It is wise to keep silent when one has nothing good to say, but it is always honest to speak the truth even when it hurts and others are offended by it. So, I choose honesty over wisdom in this regard and will honor silence no more. This prejudice of the last century is alive and prevalent today, and it is no secret that we have made no efforts to conceal it. Those beliefs which lie in the supremacy of race and the oligarchy of faith have you shamelessly exalted beyond all reason and human decency; accordingly, you have vilified and demagogued all those who happen to be different than yourselves.

Yet, despite all this, against the grain of inherent bias came those courageous heroes who strived for nothing more than equality and social justice. However, this did not sit well with the majority of you and offended your sense of pride and patriotism; therefore, have you sought only to drive a wedge between yourselves and them. "Those who are not with us are against us" was the battle cry, and with this propaganda you succeeded in galvanizing the majority to silence the minority. But the time has come and the children of this new millennium will have no more of it.

No longer will they remain silent and allow this systematic destruction of our nation and the division of its people.

TRUST

Trust and believe in me, say those who would ask something of us or seek to conceal their deceit. But those among us who are not so easily persuaded are denounced as skeptics. However, history has shown that it is much wiser to trust in one's own instincts, than to have faith in another's words. For if one's instincts are mistaken, at the very least it will lead him to the unblemished truth; whereas should one's belief in another's words and guile prove to be false, then his misguided faith is also betrayed thereby.

Though instincts are not infallible, in most cases they will more likely than not lead to the truth. However, trust in another's falsehoods only begets deception. What one knows instinctively is not an end in itself, but merely a way and a guide. Therefore, should you ever get lost along the way, believe in your instincts to guide you upon the path of truth and enlightenment.

Now, there will be times when the heavy clouds of doubt will descend and overshadow your instincts such that your reason will falter, but be not overwhelmed nor bewildered thereby. For instinct and reason (though inseparable) are not one and the same. Instinct is like an effervescent when added to a glass of water, whereas reason is what is dissolved from the concoction. Although together they provide but one solution; they are nonetheless distinct, albeit dependent upon each other. So also it is with doubt and rationalization. Therefore, always stay loyal to your instincts but hold steadfast in your reason. For even though as a consequence of doubt your judgment might waver, by trusting in your instincts and following your reason you will thus be able to rationalize your way to the right conclusion.

DECEPTION

What is deception? but the unconscionable abuse and mockery of the honesty, good faith, and sincere dedication of others. For those born of good faith and honesty (through their dedication to whatever cause) will always be the advantageous targets and bounty of the deceivers. Therefore, one must always be on a constant vigil lest he fall prey to these vile and unscrupulous predators.

Honesty, good faith, and dedication see things through the prism of pure and innocent eyes. Honesty, good faith, and dedication have always reached out to embrace the beloved, the needy, and less fortunate. It is in this humility and compassion where the traps for the unwary are set. For humility and compassion have always been mistaken for weakness, and viewed upon as an open invitation to deception.

Pity, that honesty is no longer considered a virtue amongst the masses and oftentimes the object of ridicule and scorn; that compassion and humility have been reduced to no more than a laughable trait, reserved only to those who have not yet ascended to the heights of arrogance and pomp; that sincere dedication to a worthy cause, in its docile simplicity, is doomed to fail if it does not fall into the collective pool of that which is stored in the mainstream of today's political thought. But even as recorded cataclysmic events have reversed the course of mighty rivers, so also will the power of the honest, compassionate, and humble few stem the tide of these deceivers and they shall be no more.

OF THE THREE VICES OF MAN

I have learned that there are but three vices in life that man must avoid to survive here on this earth: chronic substance abuse, degenerate gambling, and excessive womanizing. All of these three share a common thread which carries with it: financial repercussions, adverse health effects, and loss of character, which ultimately leads to self-destruction and failure. However, only the last has an additional characteristic uncommon to the others which is called: *heartbreak.* For in this process of multiple partners and romance, it is inevitable that someone always ends up "on the outside looking in," and that is a very desperate and lonely place to be.

I have witnessed first-hand the damage and devastation brought about by these vices. Each has its *manic* and *depressive* state upon the body, and therein lie the traps. For in order to maintain that high, euphoric sense of being which the actor perceives as his ultimate goal, he must (by necessity) continue in one or more of these individual pursuits at all costs; to this end he thereby avoids that which he detests most about himself: the *depressive* state.

Understanding the hidden motivation which is at the root of these vices is the first step towards rehabilitation. In trying to overcome bad habits one must not only abstain from his destructive ways, but also define and conquer oneself. For the self wants nothing more than to be understood. In the self lies all feelings, hopes, fears, and desires; however, we are helpless to control these emotions unless we first learn how to manage them.

How do we accomplish this? one might ask. By *not* following our basic instincts where experience has taught us that it would be harmful and unwise to do so; however, to trust in those same instincts when (with the aid of knowledge and reason) we have come to know what is in our best interest; last and most importantly: through understanding and wisdom, to make those hard choices which lead to a safe and more healthier lifestyle.

RELIGIOUS PREFERENCE

Having accepted the quest for truth as our mission here on earth one must consider all that has heretofore been given to us as religious doctrine. We have been shown the way of many faiths, each one presumed to be the true denomination to the exclusion of all others. But this cannot be; for does not the creator of all things unconditionally love all that it creates? Surely, the mother who gives birth to twins at the time of delivery does not hold a preference of one over the other; accordingly, so it is with faith: if you believe in a divine being or entity as the god of all creation, then you cannot presume that it is favorable only to the dogma and tenets of your religion.

For what is religion? but that faith which has been handed down to us through the generations. Once there was this belief in a divine creator of whom the scribes and others wrote down all that they had presumably seen and heard. From this was developed a protocol, wherein those who chose to follow these teachings were compelled to adhere to the principals and doctrine of those faiths.

But there were earlier times and other beliefs long before this; when a people also practiced in devout fashion such things as human sacrifices made in honor of their deity, which when viewed under contemporary standards are considered to be nothing more than barbaric rituals. In either case, what the believers of the day conceived to be a devotion to their creator in the name of religion was only that which the wisdom of the time had taught them.

Yet, it remains today: through this same devotion coupled with ignorance and fear of the unknown, man still consecrates his religion superior to the beliefs and faiths of all other men. Could he but overcome this audacity and sense of grandiosity he would soon discover that the true essence of faith is not confined in the subjective self, but rather springs eternally from the infinite well of selfless objectivity. This very well (though deep and wondrous) reposes in all of us. While there are many who have opened their hearts wide unto it and have witnessed its unknown powers, yet there still remain those others who are just too fearful and tepid to drink from its waters.

FAITH OF OUR FATHERS

I have been ostracized from the faith of family and friends because I do not subscribe in the afterlife to which my ancestors and contemporaries have so devoutly believed. Would that I could have such faith my life would be much less difficult to bear. But such is not the case, and so I am compelled to explain and defend my position in this matter.

My devout family and friends would have us believe that after our time has expired here on earth there exists an afterlife, wherein we shall all be reunited and engage with our loved ones who have long since passed from this life into another form of existence. Though admittedly unknown and unable to define just what that existence is, we are nonetheless compelled by faith to believe in it. So I must surmise, following this logic: they would have me understand that in such an afterlife I would be doing things like playing poker with my mother, ingesting spirits with my father, and at the same time reminiscing together about our past life on earth.

What we have been taught throughout the ages about the concept of "eternal life everlasting," although easy to believe is much harder and difficult to explain. It has always been said: an upright and righteous life here on earth is the key to "eternal life everlasting." This, however, is but a fiction and contradiction in terms. Because *life* is for the *living* and exists in the here and now; while death, which follows, leads only to that which at best is what most would hope for: *eternity*.

So the question as I understand it to be is: not what is "eternal life everlasting," but what is *eternity*? On this I believe we can all agree. Though reasonable minds may differ as to the answer, I would conclude by simply stating that I personally do not know. Of course, many will tell you that they do know the answer to this mystery, and would even attempt to give an explanation as to the bases of their opinions. However, the truth of the matter is: that their opinions are not founded upon personal knowledge, but reflect only a mere synopsis of the thoughts and drawn out conclusions which they have sketched from their faith.

HEAVEN'S GATES

What is *heaven*, and how and where shall we find it? I have oftentimes heard many people speak of *heaven* as though they understood the truth and meaning behind the concepts of which they speak. However, their words form not the basis of their knowledge, but are merely the conclusions of their understanding; they amount to little more than the sincere manifestations of their highest hopes and desires.

Even though through due diligence and hard work, it is conceivable that one can shape to a probable degree of certainty one's future here in this life; conversely, it cannot be even remotely presumed that you can fashion for yourself a world which lies in the afterlife. For that power rests not in the wisdom of the living, but rather in the mystery of death.

Though *heaven* is believed by many to be a remittance and reward for good behavior here on earth; this is, at best, but half the truth. Assuming for the sake of argument that there exists a *heaven*, it still begs the question: what exactly is it and how and where shall we find her? *Heaven* is not what you in your wildest and most creative dreams would fashion it to be; consequently, if it exists at all, it is something preordained which lies beyond your power and control. In truth, *heaven* is but a fantasy of the mind created only in a hope for the future; it is whatever you conceive it to be while you are amongst the living, but beyond your reach at the time of death.

PART IV

THE AMERICAN PATRIOT

Patriotism seems to be quite in vogue in this country today. Almost everyone is extremely proud to wrap themselves about with the American flag. In fact, congress not so long ago even coined a piece of legislation calling it the "Patriot Act." Of course, it could have named it something more appropriate such as the *Homeland Security Act*. Nevertheless, it chose to use the word *Patriot* so as to send a subliminal message to those who might have concerns about its far reaching implications into the invasion of privacy, and the Constitution's 4th Amendment proscriptions against unreasonable search and seizures.

You see, the insertion of the word *Patriot* into this act was intended to intimidate and silence those who knew better and saw it for what it really was. However, during the tumultuous time after the 911 attacks on American soil the country was in turmoil, and the government played upon the fears of the people. This fear was so extreme, that should any of the politicians have balked and voted their conscience, they would have been ostracized from the uninformed opinion of the main stream and denounced as weak and unpatriotic. Thus, finding themselves caught between a rock and a hard place, they made the regrettable choice of putting their careers before their country which, in the final analysis, proved not to be in the best interest of the American people.

As if this were not bad enough, they also took advantage of the good faith and sincere patriotism of the American people when (through trumped up propaganda) they sold them a bill of goods that put our troops in harm's way by sending them to war in the Middle East. This was the utmost betrayal of the people which (in their anxiety and terror) they never saw coming. The government subsequently engaged in a massive recruitment campaign to seek the enlistment of people from all walks of life to serve in the armed forces. Many of these men and women were induced to sign up for numerous reasons, all of which had at least a sense of duty and patriotism attached to it. So it came to pass, that many would be maimed and die in this effort.

Meanwhile, the Federal Reserve continued to print up currency and amass huge debt; only to enrich the wealthy corporations who, as it turned out, had monopolized the war machine at the expense of the government. These entities insinuated themselves upon the government, and by virtue of no bid contracts were brazenly permitted to enter into the national defense arena without restraint.

Alas, my friends, this is what regrettably masquerades around today as American Patriotism: to enrich the corporations through the sacrifice of human life; to proudly salute the flag and rise for the National Anthem; to remember to thank every veteran for his service; to willingly forfeit your constitutional rights so that you can feel safe and sleep well at night, all under the guise of *Patriotism*.

It is to the new millennials that I now wish to speak, for there are many things that you may not yet have heard concerning the true patriots of the past. You see, there was a time not so long ago when many servicemen returning from war in the Far East were welcomed home with little or no fanfare, and with much less enthusiasm. In fact, many of them were vilified and looked upon as no better than savages.

What happened my friends, that has caused such a revolution of ideals and reversion of thought? Well, let me begin with a short piece of history that I hope might put this into perspective. Beginning with World War Two, there existed a sentiment of unrest and sacrifice which had permeated the country; it was shared by all Americans and most of the civilized nations, who balked at the idea of some mad and vile dictator threatening to conquer the entire free world.

Here at home people felt the repercussions of that which was happening abroad by such simple things: like the ban on sliced bread so as to preserve precious metals for the making of weaponry; or schoolchildren being released from their studies early in the afternoon, to work in the fields as replacements for many of the adults who were conscripted to serve in the armed forces.

Many men who were not serving in the military for whatever reason, and women who were otherwise capable of working were employed in the munitions industry of the war machine. Everyday life was contingent upon the progress of the war over seas. Whether the lights would be turned on at night, or when evening curfews would take effect was determined by the advancement of the enemy abroad.

The culmination of this dreadful time in our history was realized when the war ended; accordingly, the many innocent people of an historical faith who survived the inhuman, despicable, death camps were liberated, and the free world could once again breathe a sigh of relief. With this victory came the return of our servicemen who (through their sacrifice and patriotism) enjoyed a much deserved homecoming filled with pomp and glory.

Shortly thereafter, there came another engagement overseas in Korea where approximately 53,000 men were killed in the brief period of five years. This war was not as popular as its predecessor, and those survivors had received much less of a welcome home. In fact, so little mention was made of this war that it is heralded as “the forgotten war”; somewhere lost in time between the memory of World War Two and the Vietnam War.

Then came the next conflict in our history which, by many, was believed to be an unjust engagement and divided the country. It is this war, where the true patriots of different stripes were the unsung heroes of their time. First, there were the conscripts, mostly young Americans between the ages of 18 and 21. These heroes were the backbone of this war effort in the Far East. Most of them (after their basic combat training) were each handed small arms weapons and dispatched into the jungle to search and destroy the enemy. Many of them would have preferred to stay here and pursue their young dreams of one day getting a decent job, owning a home, and raising a family of their own.

However, this was not to be: in a relatively short period of 10 years more than 58 thousand of them would be sacrificed. Somewhere during this time (when the casualties were mounting) the next group of American patriots emerged. Even though with the utmost sincerity and best-interest of the country at heart, there still existed a division among these forgotten heroes that caught the attention of the American people.

There was one camp that believed the war effort to be so unjust, that it despised anything or anyone associated with it. Unfortunately, this included even those young men who had survived their tour of duty, and were lucky enough to be reunited with their loved ones here at home. However, their return was not to be like the pomp and celebration enjoyed by their predecessors of World War Two, nor even the quiet indifference that welcomed home those survivors of the "forgotten war." These young men of the Vietnam War (through no fault of their own) were disrespected for their service to their country and even spat upon by these American patriots.

There also existed that other camp of American patriots, whose movement was dedicated solely to the peaceful protest of what they perceived to be an unjust war. Little mention is made of these young heroes, and those like them, who gave their lives at Kent State University for a cause they so deeply cared about. These are the ones that the American patriots of today have totally disregarded and forgotten; as if their lives were meaningless, and not worthy of the dignity and respect they deserve. So, to those amongst you who are proud to adorn yourselves with the colors of red, white, and blue, and proclaim a patriotic sense of duty to god and country would I respectfully say only this: there is much you have forgotten and still so much more you have yet to learn.

CAPITALISM

"Capitalism is a good thing," so say all the capitalists and it is well that they should. They have prospered and so life has been good to them. You have often been told: America is the greatest country on earth and this is because of capitalism. However, I believe that if we are indeed a great country it is not due to riches and power, but rather because we live in a democratic society. For greatness has never been synonymous with wealth, and true power lies not in the measure of dollars and cents.

Today's culture is structured such that currency is necessary for survival. In order that a people may live, it must depend upon currency as its means of sustenance. This, in itself, is not a bad thing; however, there is still much to be desired. Be that as it may, please understand that capitalism is not indispensable to a free society as many would suggest; however, democracy by its very definition is. For in a true democracy, it is the will of the people that govern and determine how their needs should be fulfilled. Whereas the concept of capitalism (though bolstered as necessary to a free and democratic republic) is really little more than a medium of self enrichment; it serves merely as compensation to those many successful entrepreneurs and investors who have taken calculated risks, and to whom it has served well.

Having spoken in this manner regarding capitalism, do my words advocate socialism or the denunciation of all capitalists? Absolutely not! What I would prefer is a fairness doctrine that is by no means less favorable to the rich, but rather does not discriminate against the poor. For such is the status of capitalism today. The wealthy thrive off the sweat and tears of the working class who seek only to survive. Yet, their toil and labor serves merely as a life jacket that keeps them afloat, and prevents them from sinking into the depths of misery and despair which all too many of the poor must still endure.

But it does not have to be this way. The earth has an abundance of resources that are sufficient to satisfy the needs of all its inhabitants. To the capitalists I would say only this: in order to make America the greatest country on earth and the concept of capitalism work for everyone as you so profoundly advocate, it is only necessary that you execute this sacred trust which has been given you in an evenhanded manner. Lastly, forget not to fairly compensate and justly reward those whose labor and good will have served to satisfy your needs, and has transformed what was once a dream into that which has now become a reality.

THE ALMIGHTY DOLLAR

Oftentimes has it been said: “money makes the world go around.” Also, have I heard such things as: “money is the root of all evil.” To be sure, though a contradiction in terms, both axioms are a fair and accurate account of the state of the world of finance today. Let me begin to try and reconcile this apparent conflict with a brief explanation of what is the definition of *money*.

Historically, *money* was the term that defined those precious metals such as gold and silver, which were used as a medium of exchange for the bargain and transfer of goods and services. However, today, that paper which you think of as *money* is not *money*; it is merely an inflated currency with little intrinsic value. It was near the end of World War Two when *money* in this country (and other allied nations) became that paper currency whose value was to be measured in gold. In other words, every note printed by the Federal Reserve of the United States had its monetary equivalent stored in gold reserves; thus, each dollar was accounted for in accordance with the market price of gold which, at the time, was set at $35.00 per ounce. These other allied nations unanimously came together, and (following this plan) agreed to structure their currency based upon the value of the U.S. dollar, so that the world economy would stabilize and be tethered to the single gold standard.

Now, there came a time in 1971 when the President (by executive order) instructed the Federal Reserve to back off the gold standard; consequently, it was then allowed to print as much currency as was needed by the treasury, to be loaned to the government in exchange for interest bearing IOU's. This process facilitated the government's ability to borrow and spend, without regards as to whether or not there was enough gold reserves to support this massive infusion of currency. It is common knowledge, since that time, that currency has been inflated to such a degree and extent that the more dollars that are printed the less its value. Such being the case, the simple fact of the matter is: that currency is no longer the equivalent of *money* as that term had been historical defined.

Today's currency (when measured against the gold standard of the past) amounts to nothing more than the *fiat* of the Federal Reserve to print as many worthless dollars as it wishes; accordingly, these notes are then exchanged for interest bearing loans to the government which, by the way, cannot be repaid unless it incur future debt to satisfy its past obligations. It follows: that under these questionable practices, any economist worth his salt today will tell you that this methodology and artifice is a recipe doomed for disaster.

In any event, that currency today which you think of as *mone*y really serves nothing more than the quid pro quo of the producer and seller of goods for profit, or the remuneration for the rendition of personal services for value. In either form of transfer; the purchaser of the product or the recipient of the labor, pays in currency for the goods received or the services rendered. Thus, it is true that "money makes the world go around."

But this description of *money* as that which "makes the world go around," though sound in theory, is not the end of the analysis and does not address *money* when depicted as "the root of all evil." The hard truth of the matter is: that *money*, in whatever form, has always been in the civilized world absolutely necessary to survival; consequently, without it there is little hope that anything other than misery and suffering would ensue.

However, it is not this basic human need for *money* that is inherently evil, but rather the insatiable greed of man rooted in the lust for riches is what oftentimes brings out the unspeakable and worst in him. I would therefore suggest that you consider *money* as a mere extension of the body, something *sacred* in and of itself. For when engaged in this transfer of currency in exchange for food, goods, and services, it should not be unlike any other human function necessary for the sustenance and maintenance of life.

Alas, even as there have been so many other things on this earth that man in his arrogance and ignorance has defiled, so also has he failed to act with currency in accordance with the dignity and respect it commands. Henceforth, let your pursuits and management of the "Almighty Dollar," whatever its intrinsic value, serve no other purpose than to provide for your daily needs, and insure a sense of hope and security for the future of your children.

PUBLIC HEALTH CARE

Much has been debated these days about the healthcare of our citizens and how we as a society should be responsible for it. The focal point of this topic always begins with and turns on that industry called insurance. Simply stated: the quality of healthcare in America is based upon what one can afford. Some say, like all things, this is only fair and just. Others, however, take the position that healthcare is a basic human right and not a privilege.

Obviously, due to the great advances of medicine here in the 21st century human life can be prolonged and premature death avoided. However, if all the research and development in this field is to be utilized to its greatest extent, then its advancement and achievements must be provided indiscriminately across the wide spectrum of the rich and poor alike.

Were it not for the high costs of research, development, and training of our healthcare professionals, the practice and delivery of medicine would be more affordable. However, there would always remain those who would still lack access to it. But tell me: if we can afford to subsidize foreign countries, expend fortunes on the war machine, and pursue the human exploration of outer space; why is it that we cannot manage to take care of our own sick and needy here at home when it comes to healthcare?

I have often listened to those who are in public office advocate for our less fortunate; yet their words, laudable as they may be, are hollow and fall far short of their goals. Also, there are these others who unabashedly never seem to tire of saying (though not in words): *I have it because I earned it, and your problems are not my concern.* Yet today, the sad truth of the matter still remains: that even these who have amassed their great wealth from the labor of their employees, and those others elected to serve the rich and poor alike; nonetheless have gained their fortunes and prestige off the sweat and tears of the very people upon whom they have now turned their backs.

I would now ask you: is this justice for all or only the privileged few? Why can you not find it in your hearts: those of you who have realized your great wealth off the backs of the working class, and you others who were elected to serve indiscriminately yet advocate with empty words; to deliver a means to provide this basic need to the people who can least afford it? To you in the insurance industry I would counsel only this:

there is still enough time to find a better way that you can profit from your business model, and at the same time extend your benefits to all those in need.

THE NEW REPUBLIC

The time is at hand for man to redeem the past and fulfill his mission here on earth. Change will come to the Republic though not from it. For the Republic is but the collective thought of the many instilled by the few. When that few is the wealthy and privileged, the status quo only benefits the wealthy and privileged. It is the individual who shall come one day and liberate the Republic from the status quo.

He shall come to rectify all the wrong that has long oppressed the people. The people shall rise under his tutelage, and from the people a new and free Republic shall be formed. Not a Republic that serves only the interests of the rich and powerful, but an independent Republic: "by the people and for the people." Thus, "the restoration of the earth" shall be the objective of this new and free Republic; let this new and free Republic's goal be to serve only the needs of *all* its inhabitants.

For too long has that reckless institution which we call government failed to perform the work it was entrusted with and designed to do. Instead, what it has long last achieved is only to make a mockery out of our system of democracy. This elected congress has (for the past quarter of a century) strived only to create chaos; consequently, what has prevailed is not unity but rather division. There was a period of time not so long ago during my life when both parties worked together for the greater good, and in this spirit of compromise many wonderful things were accomplished.

However, those days are long gone; consequently, what we are left with today are these so called public servants who are truly in-themselves something astonishing and rare and to behold. Have you not had the opportunity to see how they legislate? It is never a debate anymore about the substantive issues that face this great nation, nor even how they expect to resolve them. Only that sophomoric approach coupled with those caustic attitudes, in which they choose to attack and demonize one another in accordance with their political views and party affiliation. So, when it comes to a vote on a presidential appointment or some other piece of legislation that would be a victory for the proponent and benefit the American people as a whole, the opposite side (depending on the majority) will either refuse to vote it out of committee or, if so voted, filibuster until it is stalled and goes away without ever seeing the light of day.

Sadly, my friends, this vile and despicable conduct on the part of your representatives; mostly those who have graduated and received their credentials from the statehouses in this country wherein they served: is not only spiteful when based upon party lines; nor shameful when designed to undercut legislation that would benefit the nation as a whole; nor even disrespectful when it would sacrifice the integrity of a presidential nominee simply by denying him or her an up or down vote on competency; but (most reprehensibly) a flagrant disservice to the people of this country who pay their salaries, and a slap in the face to the Constitution of the United States which they took a solemn oath to uphold and defend.

As if this betrayal were not bad enough, each and every one of these tactical obstructions is countenanced today as an acceptable means of doing the people's business; justified as part and parcel of that practice which we call "politics as usual."

But I say unto the millennials of this new Republic (which is the birthright of your offspring) that the time has long since passed for such folly and gamesmanship; this hypocrisy and madness which has heretofore governed shall be one day but an embarrassment of the past, buried in the dung heap of gridlock and failure. No longer shall the future of the children of this new millennium be dependent upon nor suffer the adverse consequences and mismanagement of their predecessors.

EPILOGUE

Alas, my friends, the time has come for us to pull up the stakes, dismantle our tents that we have pitched together, and say our last goodbyes. As always, this has never been an easy task for me although I have done it many times. Yet, as sad a day as this may be, nonetheless must we part. Let us now take leave of one another not in sorrow nor burdened by heavy hearts, but rather with a sense of gratitude and in the spirit of peace and good will; such that what little we may have achieved here might not have been in vain. For what good would it serve your faith and my needs here on earth, if all that you can remember of me from this short period of time we spent together be clouded with an aura of sadness and regret. I believe it much more beneficial and gratifying for you to think only of the future of your children; at the end of the day that is all that really matters.

Remember, though many have come before me, there will be others who shall follow. Although I cannot predict the content of the message of those who are yet to be, I can say with an abundance of confidence that many of those who had come heretofore had not your best interest at heart. But I am convinced nonetheless, that each and every one of my predecessors and contemporaries who taught me had envisioned something for the future greater than themselves. A phenomenon that only men of sound reason and the utmost integrity possess: the gift of wisdom with which they have been endowed, and are obliged to give freely and indiscriminately across the board to both the rich and poor alike.

Forget not, that it was I who chose to come to you; only with the slightest hope and strongest desire that you might listen, and one day awaken to the realization that all that has been heretofore shown us may, at best, only amounted to but half the truth. However, even as half a loaf of bread is better than nothing at all, you millennials and your offspring still deserve much better. It is for this reason only that I begged your audience, so that we might come together one last time and seek to find a better way.

But if my words and ideals have fallen short of that goal, then so be it. For what I have critiqued of the past and suggested for the future, is not unlike the aspirations of the winemaker who (after the harvest of summer) has gathered his grapes for the winepress and patiently awaits the spirits of winter. So it follows: whatever I have said must not be taken as a mandate or some law to be carved in stone; it should be understood as merely the desires and expectations of a man whose memories of yesterday and hope for tomorrow, which have patiently germinated beneath the soil over time shall one day break ground and bear fruit.

Yet, be that as it may, the grounds upon which we once built our highest hope that have shaped our dreams (though uninhabited for the moment) still exist for the children of tomorrow who shall come one day and erect their own abodes, and the foundation of these homes shall be much more permanent and stationary than those transitory dwellings of ours which have preceded them. Forget not, "the teacher whose pupil does not surpass his greatest achievements and expectations has failed in his endeavors as an educator," and so it is with us. We must teach and educate in such a manner that these students of ours shall accomplish and achieve far more than what we could have ever imagined for ourselves, even in our wildest dreams.

But if we can do no more than just plant the seed in fertile soil, then we too will have fallen short of our goal as precursors of the future. For what is still lacking to the seed is water and to the soil sunshine. Just as water is the nutrient that refreshes all living things and sunshine the warmth and radiance that sustains them, so also would I have you consider knowledge as the nutrient of the soul and sunshine the enlightenment of the spirit. Then when you release these future millennials out into the world that awaits them, their roots will be well grounded and their branches exalted and firm. Unshakeable shall be their will, and unyielding the spirit; accordingly, they shall achieve with amazing ease all that we have envisioned for them as our goals for the future.

Also, from the sacred memory of those long departed of which I have spoken, it was only through their love and devotion that I was able to gather the courage and fortitude to bring this message to you. For they would have wanted nothing more than to be certain upon their death, that all those who followed would realize the American dream that they had envisioned for future generations. So it came to pass, that from this understanding and belief in them, I sought only to deliver what was truly their legacy destined to be bestowed upon each and every one of you.

Though as hard as a man tries, he has not the power alone in himself to cure all the ills of society. All he can and must do is strive to convince others in a way which is not meant that they should follow the teachings he sets forth, but rather to instill in them such confidence that through their own self knowledge and understanding they are capable of acquiring those skills sufficient to effect change not only in themselves, but also in their neighbors and all others who are willing to listen.

When I came to you it was not for the purpose that you would adhere to my doctrine as truth, but only that you might consider what little I had to offer for its content. For truth is a variable that it is contingent upon the context of the matter stated; accordingly, when the proposition offered is susceptible of two or more interpretations, its truth will be determined from the content in which you have understood it to be. So must it be with everything that I have said, and I would strongly recommend that you should take each and every bit of it with a wholesome grain of salt.

For is not the root of the problem that faces us today, *that* arrogance which emanates from all those who claim to have the whole truth and nothing but the truth? And is not *this,* the very guile and deception which has gotten us into trouble in the first place? Belief and faith in others should always be undertaken with great circumspection and caution; history has repeatedly shown that not everyone is who he claims to be, nor every proposition that has been set forth to serve the needs of the people proved to be in their best interest.

I recall from a very long time ago, that your forefathers had laid out a vision for the future of this great nation that was to benefit all people notwithstanding their faith or national origin. It was drafted under the dogma of the First Amendment of the Constitution of the United States, wherein there was to be a separation of church and state and the people would be free to assemble and petition the government for redress of their grievances. But when one faith over time becomes the dominant curriculum of a people, that is where the pull of gravity comes into play. It is in this undercurrent of the majority that all others are swept to the wayside, where they are left with little or nothing to contribute to the political process.

When it comes to national origin, there has always existed that prejudice wherein the majority who claimed their citizenship as "first in time is first in right," discriminated against all other immigrants who followed; albeit, under the same lawful policy of entry. Yet, these early immigrants had but one thing in common which persists even unto this day: a false perception that this country is theirs alone as a matter of right. However, (as history will someday bear out) they are profoundly mistaken. For the children of this new millennium have already shown a disposition to eschew these unconscionable policies of the past, and challenge those practices of today which have any tendency whatsoever to discriminate in any way, shape, or form.

So, I say unto you children of the future: that the American dream which was the standard bearer of the hopes and aspirations of your parents and grandparents is still alive and well today. It is only these last vestiges of bigotry and other abominations of the past that remain to be snuffed out. Now, it is left to you new millennials to make sure that the toil and labor of your ancestors should not have been undertaken in vain.

With this let us bid our last farewell; in the hope that tomorrow will bring to the light of day those evils of the past which have been for so long buried in the annals of the last century, such that they shall dissipate before the face of the next rising sun and be no more. For the time for change has patiently run its course and shall wait no longer. Have you not heard it once said: "that if not you, then who, and if not now, then when?" So it is with this last bit of counsel that I shall leave you.

For even now, as the longevity of the status quo is caving in upon itself (having long outlived its usefulness and inevitable collapse), so too have I lingered here amongst you perhaps a bit while longer than I should have. Be that as it may; though one cannot escape the inevitable hands of time, I can nonetheless take comfort in knowing that what has been entrusted to you will be in good hands. Having said this, I shall go peacefully and without regret; believing in that abiding faith which you have shown me; knowing that through your courage and wisdom you will shape the future of this great country; thus illuminating the contours of the new millennium not only for yourselves, but also for your children and their lineage.

www.ingramcontent.com/pod-product-compliance
Lightning Source LLC
Chambersburg PA
CBHW070625310726
48982CB00001B/172

* 9 7 8 0 9 9 8 6 2 4 7 5 4 *